From Faraway Places

by MABEL O'DONNELL *and* RONA MUNRO

NISBET

 0 7202 1008 9

CONTENTS

Marco lived here.

ITALY

Marco and the Donkey Cart

Grandfather and Marco

The donkey cart was finished. There it stood in the dusty road in front of the little white cottage where Marco lived with his grandfather.

Marco and his grandfather had been working on the cart for a long time. Every evening, when the day's work was finished, they had painted a little more.

Now Marco and his grandfather stood looking at their cart. Their eyes shone and their faces were happy. They could hardly believe that they had really made it all by themselves.

The donkey cart was beautiful. It was not very big, but it was big enough to carry both Marco and his grandfather. It was big enough to carry ten times as many bundles of wood as they could carry on their backs.

Every morning Marco and Grandfather used to walk up the dusty road to the woods outside the little village where they lived. All morning they gathered the dry branches from under the trees and put them into bundles. Then, with the bundles on their backs, they walked into town and sold the bundles of firewood in the market.

6

The early morning sunlight made all the different colours of the donkey cart look better than ever.

Marco had helped to paint the cart. He had painted the wheels and the long shafts. But only Grandfather could paint the pictures on the sides and back of the cart.

On each side of the cart Grandfather had put two pictures. On one side he had painted a picture of a puppet show, like the puppet show that had come to the village a year before.

Next to the puppet show was a picture of people dancing. They were dancing in a market place very like the one in Marco's own village.

On the back of the cart Grandfather had painted a picture of a shepherd. The shepherd stood on a hill, looking down at his sheep in the green field below.

On the other side of the donkey cart were the two pictures Grandfather liked best. In one picture some boys and girls were singing. In the other two boys were playing tunes on their bagpipes.

These were Grandfather's favourite pictures because he liked music. In the evenings, when their work was done, Marco would take out his bagpipes and play one tune after another. Grandfather never tired of listening.

Sometimes the other boys and girls of the village would come to the little white house and ask Marco to play for them. Then they would dance while he played.

But today Marco and his grandfather were not thinking about music. The only thing they could think of was their beautiful new donkey cart.

As they stood and looked at it, other people came to look too. The family who lived next door came out first.

What, No Donkey?

Then the village boys and girls came, and the farmers on their way to market stopped to look. They gathered round the cart, staring at the bright colours and the beautiful pictures.

One farmer had a great basket on his back. It was full of the vegetables that he was taking to sell in the market.

"How I should like to have a cart like that to carry my vegetables," he exclaimed.

Then all at once a voice from the crowd called out "Where is the donkey to pull the cart?"

Other voices in the crowd joined in. "Yes, tell us. Where is your donkey?"

Grandfather did not answer. Zi Peppi, the farmer with the basket of vegetables, looked at him in surprise.

"Have you done so much work on the cart without a donkey to pull it?" he asked.

11

Still Grandfather said nothing. Marco knew why. He remembered Grandfather's words while they worked on the cart.

"The cart is no use without a donkey to pull it. How people would laugh at us! We must earn the money for a donkey before we can use this cart."

They had worked hard for the money that Grandfather kept hidden in an old sock. But now, when they needed it most, the money was gone. Some had been spent on Marco's bagpipes. Some had been used to buy the wheels for the cart, and the paint. The rest had gone for the harness. There was no money left for the donkey itself.

Marco and Grandfather had talked about it only last night. From now on they would work harder than ever. They would carry more branches from the woods and sell more bundles in the market. They would earn enough money to buy a donkey of their own.

Grandfather ran his hand over the side of the cart, and smiled at Marco. "Soon," he said to the crowd. "Soon Marco and I will have a donkey."

Zi Peppi just stared at Grandfather. He could not believe what he heard.

"Soon!" he exclaimed. "How will you ever find enough money for a donkey? Your cart will stand here in the sun for years while you and the boy break your backs carrying firewood."

Suddenly someone in the crowd called out with a laugh "Why don't you give them a donkey, Zi Peppi?"

"I! I give them a donkey?" cried Zi Peppi.

"Yes," another voice answered. "Why not give them Serafina, that hard-working donkey you bought from the puppet show people last summer?"

Everyone laughed loudly at that, even Grandfather and Marco.

Everyone in the village knew about Serafina the donkey. She would not work at all. She never even left her field. Zi Peppi could not sell her, because no buyer could get her to move. When anyone asked about her, Zi Peppi's face would turn red and cross.

Now an old white-haired man stepped out of the crowd. He smiled as he looked at the cross Zi Peppi.

"Tell me, Zi Peppi," he said, "have you had any luck in finding someone to buy that donkey from you?"

Zi Peppi shook his head.

"No," he said. "No luck at all."

"Then why not give her away?"

"How can I give her away? Didn't I spend good money on that donkey?" said Zi Peppi.

"Aren't you spending more good money on the food she eats while she does no work?" asked the old man.

"You are right!" exclaimed Zi Peppi. "Each day I grow more tired of feeding a lazy useless donkey."

"Then give her away," said the old man, "and save the money you pay for her food."

Zi Peppi's face turned redder than ever. Everyone was laughing at him. For a minute or two he stood thinking things over.

No, Thank You!

"All right! It's a bargain. Serafina is yours," he said at last, turning to Grandfather. "All I ask in return is a ride to market every morning with my basket of vegetables."

"Bravo, Zi Peppi!" shouted the crowd.

"Thank you, no!" cried Grandfather. "What can I do with a donkey that will not work? I have no money to waste on her."

"Oh, Grandfather!" shouted Marco. "Please take her."

17

Grandfather shook his head. "If she won't work for her master, she won't work for us, Marco," he said.

"Please, Grandfather," begged Marco. "Perhaps she isn't really lazy. Perhaps she only needs something she likes to do. I'm sure she will like working for us."

Everyone laughed loudly at this, even Zi Peppi.

"Well," said Grandfather with a smile. "We will give Serafina a chance. Zi Peppi's farm is on our way to the woods, so we can stop there when we go to gather our sticks."

Marco remembered that Serafina liked to eat.

"We must take some oats with us for Serafina," he said.

"Don't bother," laughed Zi Peppi. "She has already eaten today. She had enough for two hard-working donkeys."

"We can give her something after she has done her work," said Grandfather.

"Then I'll take something else that she will like," said Marco, as he ran back into the little white house.

A minute later he was back with the beautiful red donkey harness on his arm. The mirrors on the harness straps sparkled brightly in the sunlight.

19

The wise old man looked first at the red harness, and then at Marco.

"Don't be surprised if Marco leads Serafina straight out of your field," the old man said to Zi Peppi. "Some boys have a way with donkeys."

Zi Peppi looked as if he did not believe a word of it.

"Go up to my field and see what you can do," he said to Marco. "The next time I see that lazy donkey I hope she has that harness on her back and is pulling this cart."

Serafina

"Good luck!" everyone called, as Marco and Grandfather started off up the road to Zi Peppi's farm.

There in the field was Serafina, the grey and white donkey. She seemed very friendly, and rubbed her nose against Marco's hand as he patted her.

"I wish I had something to give you," said Marco softly.

"Don't hurry. Take your time," said Grandfather, as he handed the harness to Marco.

Slowly Marco placed the harness on
Serafina's back. The donkey stood very
still to let him fasten the buckles. Before Marco knew how it happened, he
was finished. He could not believe how
easy it had been.

There stood Serafina, all harnessed
and ready to go. The red of the harness
was just the right colour, and all the
little mirrors sparkled in the sunlight.

"Now see if she will go to the open gate with you," whispered Grandfather.

"Come, Serafina, come," said Marco softly, as he pulled on the reins.

Serafina's ears went up, but she did not move. Marco pulled a little harder. Still Serafina did not move. He tugged as hard as he could, but she did not budge.

"It's no use," said Grandfather. "Come, Marco. We must gather firewood."

Marco let go the reins and stared at the donkey. When Serafina looked at him he knew that she liked him. Then why wouldn't she do what he wanted?

"We can't give up, Grandfather," he said. "Think of the money we shall earn if only she will help us."

Grandfather would wait no longer. While Marco tugged at the reins again, Grandfather walked out of the field.

"Come, Marco," called Grandfather. "Time is flying and there is wood to be gathered into bundles."

"Just a little longer! Please, Grandfather," called Marco. "Perhaps we can find out what Serafina wants us to do. Oh, I have it, Grandfather! I know what is wrong. Serafina has her harness on, but there is no cart. If she saw our beautiful cart she would want to work."

Grandfather laughed loudly. "How can we show her the cart if she will not go with us?" he asked.

"We can bring the cart here!" cried Marco. "Please let us try it."

"Bring the cart to the donkey!" exclaimed Grandfather. "Who ever heard of such a silly idea!"

"But when Serafina sees the cart she will come with us," begged Marco.

Grandfather turned round. "Come on then if you must have your way."

So back went Grandfather and Marco down the long road to fetch the cart.

Soon the village people saw Grandfather between the shafts of the donkey cart, pulling it slowly up the hot dusty road while Marco pushed from behind. They laughed and called to each other. Some of them made jokes about the stupid things that people did.

At last Marco and Grandfather were back at the farm, tired and hot from their long walk in the sun.

Grandfather and Marco stopped just outside the gate of the field. Inside the gate Serafina stared knowingly at the little painted cart.

"Look, Grandfather! She loves it!" exclaimed Marco.

All at once Serafina started to bray. They patted the donkey. They talked to her. They did their best to lead her out of the gate and up to the cart. But you can't make a donkey move if it doesn't want to.

Serafina went on braying loudly, but she would not budge.

"Enough is enough!" exclaimed Grandfather, when he could stand no more. "I am going to gather firewood, and you will take the harness off that stubborn, useless animal."

Marco did not say a word. He was sorry now that he had made Grandfather take that long, hot walk in the sun to bring the cart to the field.

He turned to look at the donkey. She was still braying. Grandfather would be gone for a while. Perhaps Marco could try something else before he took the harness off.

Without knowing why he did it, Marco jumped up on to Serafina's back. The donkey turned her head to stare at him. He patted her head and dug his toes into her sides. Up went Serafina's ears, and she jumped forward.

The next moment she was trotting round the field with Marco on her back.

"Bravo!" shouted Marco. "If only Grandfather were here now! You are not really lazy after all."

Marco's words made Serafina trot faster and faster. He turned her head towards the open gate. Just a little farther, and she would be out of the gate and up to the cart.

All at once Marco was flying backwards off Serafina's back. The reins slipped out of his hands, and with a great thump he landed on the hard ground.

Marco jumped to his feet, as cross as could be. By this time Serafina was back in the middle of the field, braying loudly.

"What's wrong with you?" shouted Marco. "Any other donkey would be glad to be harnessed to a cart as beautiful as ours."

Music for Serafina

Slowly and unwillingly Marco started to take the beautiful red harness off Serafina's back. He carried it back to the cart. As he was putting it in, his eyes fell on the pictures on the sides; first the dancing puppets, and then the two boys playing the bagpipes.

Marco stared at the pictures, while his eyes began to sparkle. The pictures were giving him an idea.

Back to the village he ran, faster than he had ever run before. Into the little white house, and then back up the hot dusty road to the field.

When he reached it, Grandfather was throwing a bundle of branches into the cart. He looked at Marco in surprise.

"What are you doing with those bagpipes out here?" he asked.

"I am going to play them for Serafina," answered Marco.

"You silly boy!" exclaimed Grandfather. "Who ever heard of playing bagpipes for a donkey? Now stop this nonsense. There is work to be done."

"But, Grandfather," begged Marco. "Serafina belonged to the puppet show we saw last summer. There was always plenty of music in the puppet show. Perhaps that is what is wrong with Serafina. She misses all the music."

Grandfather shook his head. He did not believe a word Marco was saying.

Marco looked over at Serafina. She had stopped braying, and was eating grass. Marco started to play his bagpipes.

As soon as Serafina heard the tune Marco was playing her ears went up. She stopped eating and lifted her head to listen. She didn't move until the music had ended.

Then Serafina walked straight out of the gate and round to the front of the cart. She turned round and backed up between the shafts. There she stood, all ready to be harnessed.

"She likes it! She likes it!" Marco shouted. "Serafina likes music as much as you do, Grandfather. Now she wants to work for us."

"If I hadn't seen it with my own eyes I would never have believed it," cried Grandfather.

In a minute or two Serafina was harnessed. Grandfather and Marco climbed into the cart. The wheels started to turn as Serafina began to trot.

Bravo, Marco!

As they were riding along, Marco and Grandfather met Zi Peppi on his way home from the market. Marco pulled the reins to stop Serafina. At first the farmer was so surprised that he could hardly speak.

"How did you get that lazy donkey out of my field?" he asked at last.

"Remember what the old man told you," answered Grandfather. "Boys do have a way with donkeys. Marco found out what Serafina wanted."

"And what was that?" asked Zi Peppi.

"Music," said Grandfather. "She is not really lazy. She just likes music."

"Music!" cried Zi Peppi. "Is that what made her work? The man who sold her to me said that she needed a little music before breakfast to make her work, but I thought he was joking."

Grandfather laughed. "He should have told you what would happen if she did not get her music," he said. "He should have told you that without music she would not budge. We will come by in the morning to take you and your basket to market."

Zi Peppi smiled. "I stick to my word," he said. "Serafina is yours from now on."

When the people saw Grandfather
and Marco come riding into the village,
they crowded round the cart, shouting
"They have a donkey for their cart.
Serafina the stubborn donkey is
working! Bravo, bravo!"

Grandfather waved and laughed.
"Play, Marco," he said. "Play a tune
for Serafina while I hold the reins."

So Marco played on his bagpipes
while Serafina trotted smartly along,
and the children's dancing feet followed
the wonderful cart down the village
street.

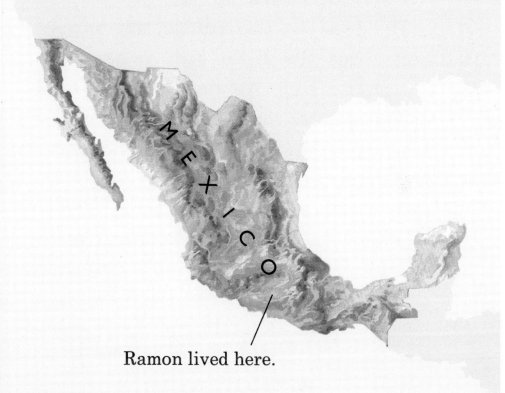

Ramon lived here.

Ramon Makes a Trade

To the Market

The road to the village was full of holes, but the little grey donkey did not miss a step. All that could be seen of him was his legs, his tail and his two long ears. The rest was hidden by the many-coloured bowls and jars that were fastened to his sides and back. Slowly and steadily the little donkey trotted along.

Ramon's father, in his old ragged serape, walked beside the donkey, holding the reins and taking care that no bowl fell and got broken. Behind the donkey walked Ramon's mother, and behind Ramon's mother walked Ramon.

In his arms Ramon carried a beautiful bowl that he had made all by himself. His eyes were on the road, for it would not do to fall and break the bowl that had taken so long to make.

"Ramon," his father called back to him. "Do you want me to put your bowl on my stall and try to find a buyer for it? It is a very good bowl."

"Thank you, no, Papa," said Ramon. For the first time he took his eyes off the road to look at the orange-coloured bowl he was carrying so carefully. It was beautiful, but he did not think that it would look so beautiful if it stood beside his father's jars and bowls.

Sandino, Ramon's father, was the best potter in the village. He was one of the best potters in all Mexico. People crowded round his stall on market days to buy water jars made by the great potter Sandino.

They would not want to buy a bowl that a boy had made. It would be difficult to find a buyer for the bowl. Perhaps no one would buy it at all.

Then suddenly a good idea came into Ramon's head.

"If no one will buy my bowl," he shouted, "I will trade it for something I want. I know just what that thing will be."

"You are a clever boy, Ramon," said his mother. "That is a good plan. Not many people at the market have money, but all of them have things to trade. What is this thing for which you will give one beautiful orange-coloured bowl?"

Ramon smiled, thinking of that something which would soon be his.

"That is a secret, Mama," he said, "and I cannot tell a secret."

Ramon's Secret

When they reached the market, Ramon left Mama and Papa at their stall and began to push his way through the crowds of people. Everyone was moving from stall to stall, looking the wares over before buying and talking loudly about the prices.

Suddenly, over the noise of shouting people and braying donkeys, Ramon heard a loud screeching voice.

"Hullo! Good-bye! Hullo! Good-bye!"
shouted the voice, louder than all the
other noises in the market.

Ramon laughed. He stood on tiptoes,
trying to see over the heads of the
people around him.

"I can hear you, Mr Parrot," he said
to himself. "I'm coming to get you. I
will give this beautiful bowl for you.
Then I will carry you home in your
cage, and teach you to say many other
things. I will keep you always, and
everyone will know that you are
Ramon's parrot."

Ramon pushed on towards the place
from which the screeching voice was
coming. Sometimes he could hardly
move for the crowd.

Once he stopped to look at a merry-
go-round. Boys and girls were riding
round and round on the coloured
ponies, laughing and calling.

Under the big round platform Ramon could see three boys about as big as himself. They were pushing hard and kicking the dust up with their feet as they worked to keep the merry-go-round turning round and round.

Ramon liked the merry-go-round very much, but it would cost a centavo to ride, and he had no money. Perhaps if business was very good Papa would give him a centavo at the end of the day.

Ramon moved along until at last he
struggled out of the crowd in front of
the stall of bird cages. There were many
empty cages on the stall, and just one
cage with a bird inside. The bird was a
little parrot with bright green feathers
and a long tail.

"Good day!" screeched the parrot.
It turned its head and looked at Ramon
with one shining eye. It moved along its
perch towards him.

The man who made the cages was
paying no attention to the squawking
bird. He was looking at Ramon's
beautiful orange bowl.

"That is a fine bowl you have there,"
he said. "It is so fine that it must be
one made by Sandino."

Ramon pushed his big hat back. A
proud look came into his eyes.

46

"Sandino the potter is my father," said Ramon, "but I made this bowl myself on my father's wheel. I mixed the colour for it too."

Things were going better than he had expected. Perhaps it would not be too difficult to make a trade.

"I will give my fine bowl for the cage and the little green parrot," he said to the man.

How the man laughed! Then he shook his head.

"That is not good business," he said with a smile. "The cage took me a long time to make. It was hard to catch the parrot in the woods. It took many weeks before the parrot learned to talk. The bowl is beautiful, but I would only trade the cage and the little parrot for six bowls like it."

Ramon looked at his bowl. The warm orange colour did not look so beautiful now. The man looked kindly at Ramon's unhappy face.

"What I would really like to have," he said, "is one of your father's green water jars. I would put it on my donkey's back and bring water from the river. For one of the green jars I will trade the cage and the parrot."

"Thank you," said Ramon. "I will see what I can do."

The Serape Weaver

Ramon turned away sadly. His father would never give one of the fine green jars for a cage with a squawking bird inside.

What Sandino the potter really needed was a new serape instead of his ragged one. He could use the serape as a coat on cold days and as a blanket on cold nights. Ramon's father would gladly give a water jar for a new serape. That would be a good trade.

Once again Ramon looked down at the orange-coloured bowl. It looked more beautiful than ever. Perhaps the serape weaver would think so too. Perhaps he was looking for a fine bowl just like this. If he would give Ramon a serape for the bowl, Ramon could give the serape to his father for a green water jar. Then he could take the jar to the man who made bird cages.

Once again Ramon made his way
through the crowds in the market
place. This time he was looking for the
weaver. At last, high above his head,
he saw a pile of serapes moving slowly
through the crowd. He waved and called
to the weaver, who did not have a stall
but was carrying the serapes upon his
head.

The weaver laughed loudly when
Ramon asked him to trade one orange
bowl for a serape.

He stopped laughing when he saw Ramon's unhappy face.

"It is a fine bowl," said the weaver, "and I would like to have it. But it is not enough to trade for one of my good serapes."

He stood there a minute, thinking.

"Here is what I will do," he said at last. "I will take in trade for one serape, your fine bowl and twenty centavos. That is not much money, but the bowl is a beautiful orange colour, and I want it because of that."

"Thank you," said Ramon. "I will see what I can do."

Poor Ramon! How could he get twenty centavos to trade for a serape? In all his life he had never had as many as twenty centavos at a time. And if he could not get a serape to trade for a green water jar, he could not trade the water jar for the parrot.

Ramon walked away with tears in his eyes. There was no one who could help him. There was nothing he could do.

"Good-bye," called the parrot from its cage on the stall.

"Good-bye, Mr Parrot," answered Ramon softly so that no one else could hear. "Wait for me! Some day I will make six beautiful bowls and mix the colours for them too. Then I will come back and get you."

Before long Ramon was back at the merry-go-round. The ponies were still going round and the boys were still pushing. Ramon wanted a ride very much, but he still had no centavo.

"Perhaps I can give my bowl for a ride," he thought. "Perhaps I can get three or four rides for the bowl. I will ride until I am dizzy and my head goes round and round too. Then I will forget all about the little parrot."

He thought of the bright eyes and the shining green feathers of the parrot which would never be his.

"How many rides will you let me have in trade for this bowl?" he asked, walking up to the owner of the merry-go-round.

The man scratched his head and considered.

"None at all," he said at last. "I can't give any rides for a bowl."

When he saw the look on Ramon's face the man started to explain.

"It's like this," he said. "I have to have centavos for rides, because I must pay centavos to the boys who push the merry-go-round. How could I pay them with a bowl? Could I break it and give a piece to each one? No, I must have centavos for rides."

"Perhaps I could push the merry-go-round," said Ramon.

"Certainly," said the man. "I always need boys to push. Get under the platform and push the merry-go-round for two rides, and I will give you one centavo. With that centavo you can buy one ride for yourself."

"Then keep my bowl safe for me, and I will do it," said Ramon.

The merry-go-round came to a stop. When it started again Ramon was under it, pushing hard.

Ramon pushed for two rides, and the man gave him one centavo. He dropped the centavo into the orange bowl.

"I will push again and earn another centavo," he said to the owner.

Ramon pushed for the rest of the morning. The hot afternoon came, and most of the people in the market place went to sleep in the shade. But the boys and girls went on riding, and Ramon went on pushing. He was very hot and quite worn out, but he went on working. He would not give up.

"I have never seen a boy who pushed so hard and so long," said the owner. "Rest a while, boy, and use one of your centavos to buy a ride."

"Thank you, no," answered Ramon.

Each time he finished pushing two rides the man gave him one centavo. Ramon dropped each centavo into the orange bowl.

Poor Ramon did not take one ride. Late in the afternoon, when everyone in the market place was awake again, he crawled out from under the merry-go-round and ran to drop the last centavo into his bowl. The pieces of money jingled together. Ramon smiled as he sat down to count them.

"Twenty-one centavos!" he cried. "It is more than enough. I must go now, but I will come back."

A Very Good Day

Once more Ramon pushed his way through the crowd, looking for the weaver. At last he found him. He gave the weaver his orange-coloured bowl with twenty centavos in it. In exchange the weaver gave him a fine serape with a bright coloured pattern.

Holding the serape high above his head, Ramon ran off to his father's stall.

"Look, Papa," he shouted. "A new serape for a ragged one."

When Ramon told his father the story Sandino was glad to take the serape.

"You have worked hard and done better business than I have today," he said. "Take my best green jar."

He put his head through the hole in the new serape. That turned it from a blanket into a fine new coat.

59

The water jar was almost as big as Ramon, and very heavy. It was hard work carrying it safely through the market to the stall of the bird cages. Ramon was thankful to set it down.

"Here is a green water jar made by Sandino the potter," he said. "Now you can fetch water from the river. In trade I will take the cage with the little green parrot."

"Good," said the man. He took down the cage and gave it to Ramon.

Ramon walked back to the merry-go-round with his parrot. He gave the owner his last centavo.

"Now I would like to buy a ride," he said with a laugh.

"But I have no boys to push! Market day is almost over, and everyone is going home," exclaimed the man.

He was a very kind man. When he saw the disappointed look on Ramon's face he knew that there was only one thing for him to do.

"It is too bad that such a hard-working boy as you should get no ride," he said. "I will push you myself."

There was hardly room for him underneath the platform, but he crawled under and began to push. Ramon was already up on a pony, holding the cage in one hand and his hat in the other. The merry-go-round started to move faster and faster.

As he rode the parrot became more and more excited.

"Hullo! Good-bye! Hullo! Good-bye!" screamed the parrot. "Hullo! Good day! Good day!"

"You are right, Mr Parrot," laughed Ramon, as the pony went round and round. "It has been a good day. A very good day indeed!"

The Pedlar of Swaffham

John Chapman
lived here.

ENGLAND

The Pedlar's Home

Many years ago there lived a pedlar in the village of Swaffham. His name was John Chapman, and he lived by himself in a tiny cottage at the end of the village. The cottage had only one room in it, and that room was so small that there was just room in it for the pedlar's bed and his table and chair. He did all his cooking in a great pot over the fire.

Roses climbed over the front of the cottage and bright flowers grew under the window. At the back there was a big garden where John Chapman grew his vegetables.

In the middle of the garden stood an old pear tree. In spring it was always white with blossom, and in autumn it carried a load of juicy pears. He liked to sit under it and listen to the birds singing.

The pedlar should have had plenty to eat from his garden. But as soon as the lettuces and carrots were well grown whole families of rabbits came in from the fields. They munched and munched until there was hardly anything left.

Then when the fruit was ripe the blackbirds flew in for their share. They ate up all the berries and pecked great holes in the pears.

The pedlar's dog would have chased the rabbits away, but the pedlar would not let him. He wouldn't even let the dog bark at the blackbirds. "They don't take much," he said, "and there is enough for us all."

The neighbours frowned and shook their heads at him. "You are a foolish fellow, John Chapman," they said. "The animals take all you grow, and you never try to stop them. One of these days you'll be hungry and have to beg for food."

John Chapman only laughed and went his own way.

The Pedlar's Pack

Whenever there was a market in one of the villages near Swaffham, the pedlar would get up early and have his breakfast before the sun was up. Then he would pull on his red woollen cap, take up his heavy pack and set off.

At the market John would look for a good place to set out his wares. If you want to know what he had in his pack, the answer is anything and everything. He had needles and pins and buttons. He had brushes and ribbons. He had toys for children and beads for their mothers.

When the market was over he would pack up his wares, call his dog and set off home to Swaffham.

As he trudged on his way a little girl might come running out to him, calling "Mr Pedlar, Mr Pedlar, I want a new hair ribbon. Have you a pretty one in your pack?"

It sometimes happened that the ribbon cost more than the little girl had.

"Never mind," the pedlar would say. "Have it now, and pay me when you are rich." Then he would help her to tie it in her hair.

Another time it might be a boy who had seen the very knife he longed for. "How much is it?" he would ask the pedlar, and then drop the knife back. "I haven't enough money to buy it," he would say sadly.

"Take it anyway, and pay me when you are rich," the pedlar would say, and feel that the boy's happy face more than paid for the knife.

The pedlar made very little money, but wherever he went he left somebody happier than before.

His neighbours thought that he was foolish to care so little about money.

"Some day you will have nothing left in your pack or your pockets," they said. "You will need money then, and where will you find it? Take our advice and mend your ways." But John took no notice of them.

If there was no fair or market John liked to sit on his doorstep in the sun. The village children would come along in twos and threes and sit down with him. They loved to listen to the stories he told of the places he had seen.

71

The years went by, and the pedlar grew older. When he walked the long roads to the fairs his legs grew weary, and he and his dog would have to sit resting by the wayside. He still gave away more goods than he sold, and his pack was almost as empty as his pockets, but John Chapman did not care.

"If my pack has less in it, it is lighter to carry," he thought, "and I would rather see happy faces round me than be a rich man."

John Chapman's Dream

One evening the pedlar trudged sadly home to his cottage. His pack was empty at last, and he had nothing to sell. His pockets were empty too. He and his dog were tired and hungry.

He looked in his cupboard, but there was only a little bread in it. He went to his pear tree to look for a pear, but there was not one left. The birds had eaten them all.

"Perhaps my neighbours were right," said the pedlar to himself. "If I had listened to their advice I might have had money in my pockets and plenty to eat in my house. Well, it is too late now."

Hungry as he was, he gave the piece of bread to his dog. Then he lay down on his bed. Soon he fell asleep, and began to dream the strangest dream he had ever had.

In his dream the pedlar was lying on his bed looking at the embers of the fire. Suddenly the door opened without a sound, and a stranger was standing in the doorway.

The stranger was a tall man in fine clothes, finer than any John had ever seen. He beckoned John with one finger, and said,

"John Chapman of Swaffham, listen to me. Get up, put on your pack, and

take the road to London. Stand in the middle of London Bridge and wait for your fortune to come to you."

Before the pedlar could ask any of the questions that were on his lips, the door closed again and the stranger was gone.

John hardly knew whether he was awake or dreaming. He jumped out of bed and opened the door, but there was nothing outside. His dog was still asleep by the fire, so he shook his head and went back to bed.

When he woke in the morning the pedlar remembered his dream, but he did not go to London.

"Only a fool would do as a dream told him," he thought. "It is a long way to London, and I am too old to walk there and back for nothing."

By the time he went to bed that night he had forgotten all about his dream. But no sooner had he fallen asleep than he saw the stranger again standing in his doorway and saying,

"John Chapman of Swaffham, listen to me. Get up, put on your pack, and take the road to London. Stand in the middle of London Bridge, and wait for your fortune to come to you."

The next day the pedlar stayed at home, but he thought about the dream for a long time. That night he had the same dream a third time, and when he woke there were no doubts in his mind.

Before the day had broken John had put on his pack and started off for London. He left his dog with a kind neighbour.

"The dream said nothing about you," he said as he patted him, "and you are too old for such a journey."

It took John Chapman four days to walk to London, and with each day he grew more weary. At last he toiled up a long hill and looked down to see London spread out below him.

On London Bridge

In all his life the pedlar had never seen so many houses or so many people. He was hard put to it to make his way through the crowds until he came to London Bridge.

There he walked to the middle of the bridge, and stood looking at the people who passed him. Not one of them looked at him. They hurried by, each thinking of his own business and not seeing the old pedlar with his dusty pack.

All day long he stood there waiting, and all the next day. As the time passed his legs grew so tired that he could stand no more, and he sat down.

In his mind he said, "You foolish old man! Here you are on London Bridge, but the fortune is still a dream. And where will you find the strength to walk home again?"

Slowly he got to his feet and started to walk off the bridge. He hardly knew where he was going.

As he passed one of the shops that lined the bridge, the shopkeeper came out and stopped him.

"I want to ask you a question, Pedlar," said the shopkeeper.

"What is it?" asked the pedlar.

"All day yesterday you stood on the bridge," said the man, "and you are here again today. What are you waiting for?"

John Chapman was not very willing to answer him, but the shopkeeper said kindly, "By your looks you have not eaten or slept well for a long time. Now there is food on my table and a good fire in my kitchen, and you shall enjoy them both if you will tell me your story afterwards."

The pedlar could not refuse that, and he gladly followed the shopkeeper into his house. There he ate his fill, and then stretched out his legs to the fire and slept.

When he woke, the shopkeeper asked his question again.

"Why do you stand on the bridge all day?"

The pedlar felt very foolish, but he answered, "I am waiting for my fortune."

"Your fortune?" exclaimed the shop-keeper. "Do you expect it to come walking up to you? Or did you hear that the streets of London are paved with gold?"

"No," said the pedlar. "I had a dream that came three nights running. I was told to go and stand on London Bridge."

"And you did as you were told?"
said the shopkeeper, and he shouted
with laughter. "Did you ever hear such
a story! Why, Pedlar, I have had a
dream three nights running too, but I
never thought of doing as it told me."

"You had a dream too?" said John
Chapman.

"Yes, indeed," said the shopkeeper. "In my dream a man came into my shop. He beckoned to me and said, 'Go to Swaffham in Norfolk, and find a tiny cottage at the end of the village. Dig under the pear tree in the garden, and you will find the gold that lies there.' Then he vanished."

He shook his head and laughed.

"Swaffham!" he said. "I don't know where it is, and I don't care. Only a foolish man would take any notice of a dream. Go home, Pedlar, and forget your dream."

"Yes," said John Chapman, "I will go home, but I don't think I shall forget my dream."

Back went the pedlar along the road to Swaffham, and never looked behind him. At last he came to his cottage, and his dog ran to meet him. He sat down under his pear tree.

The Dream Comes True

"Now what shall I do?" said John to himself. "Should I believe in another dream and dig under my pear tree? Well, I have been foolish all my life, and I am too old to change now."

He took off his pack and went for a spade. Then he began to dig under the big pear tree. It was not long before his spade struck something hard in the ground. The pedlar was excited and dug faster.

In no time at all John Chapman had uncovered a small iron chest. He broke the lock and lifted the lid. The chest was full of gold pieces.

From that day on John Chapman was a rich man, but he still lived in his tiny cottage. On market days he carried his pack to the villages round, but he gave away most of his wares. There were stories for the children, and a present for each of them.

The poor people in the country round came to know that no one ever went away from his door without help. And for his neighbours in Swaffham he built a fine new church.

Many years later, when the pedlar died, the people of Swaffham wanted his story and his kindness to be remembered. They made a statue of him with his pack on his back and his dog at his heels. Then they set it up in Swaffham, and there it stands to this day.

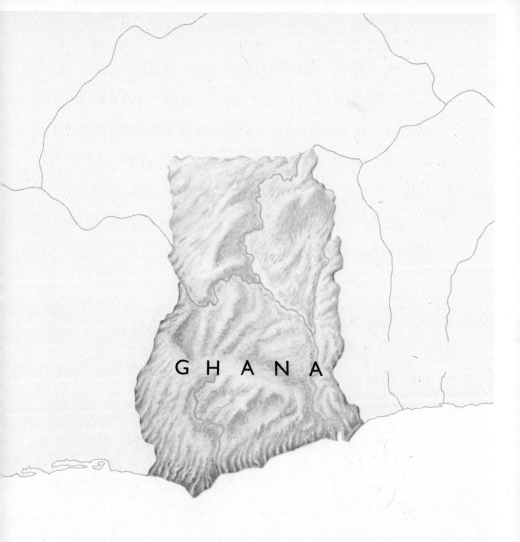

G H A N A

Why Spiders Hide
in Dark Corners

A Folk Tale from Ghana

In Ghana there are many folk tales about a strange creature called Spider. He is supposed to be a spider, but he acts like a man. He loves to eat, and he hates to work. He thinks he is clever, but at times he is stupid.

Each story about Spider explains why something happens. One story explains why the moon is in the sky. Another explains why turtles have hard shells. This story tells why spiders hide in dark corners.

Spider's Plan

Once upon a time Spider lived with his wife and his two sons in a house made of banana leaves. Not far away was the forest where the cocoa trees grew.

Behind the banana-leaf house was a garden. In it Spider and his wife planted many vegetables. Orange and banana trees grew around its edges.

When the rains came each year, the vegetables grew, and the garden was green and beautiful. The oranges and bananas ripened, and Spider and his family had all they wanted to eat.

Each day Spider's wife cooked rice and fish and vegetables and other good things in her big cooking pot. The smell of that wonderful stew made Spider's mouth water. Each day Spider went on eating until he could eat no more.

You might have thought that Spider would be satisfied, but he wasn't. Every day, as soon as the stew had disappeared, he looked around to find something for his wife to cook next. He wanted to eat most of the time when he wasn't sleeping.

As the days went by, something began to trouble Spider.

"Things are not as they should be here," he said to himself one morning. "Of all the good things in my garden, the very best things should be only for me. I must think of a way to save the best things for myself. My family can get along with the rest."

So Spider sat down under a banana tree in the garden to think. At last he had a great idea. He began to carry out his plan at once.

First he hung his head down low. Next he pretended that he could hardly walk, as he made his way back to the banana-leaf house.

"Something is wrong with me," he said to his wife. "I am not feeling well. I am very sick indeed, and I must wait no longer. I must go to the village to see the magician. Since he is wise enough to know what will happen tomorrow, next week, or even next year, he will know what is wrong with me."

"I will go with you to help you on your way," said his wife, looking at him sadly with tears in her eyes.

"You must stay where you are," insisted Spider. "If I do not go by myself, the magician will be angry."

The day was almost over before Spider returned home. His wife and his two sons were waiting near the doorway.

"My dear wife and my two sons," said Spider, shaking his head and looking as if the world had come to an end, "I have bad news for you. The magician tells me that I am very sick. No one can do anything to help me. Soon I am going to die and leave you."

"Die and leave us?" cried his wife and his two sons. "That cannot be."

It took time, but at last Spider made his family understand that what was to be would be. He was going to die, and there was nothing they could do about it. "Since I am about to die," he went on to explain, "these are the things you must do for me so that I will be happy in the next world.

"First you must dig a deep hole in the garden. Come, and I will show you. Put it here next to the spot where the biggest and ripest tomatoes grow."

Spider liked tomatoes best of all the good things that grew in his garden.

"Next you must find a box to put me in," he continued. "It must be big and have a cover that is easy to lift. Place the box in the hole, and into it put some spoons and knives and pots so that I can feed myself in the next world."

Spider's wife and his two sons carried out each order carefully.

One day, not long after this, Spider stretched out on the ground in the sun. He shut his eyes and did not move. He remembered to hold his breath when anyone came near him. In every way, he pretended that he was dead. But, of course, he wasn't.

Spider's sons, trying hard to hold back their tears, raced to the village to tell all his friends the bad news.

In no time, Spider's friends were at the door of the banana-leaf house.

Carefully they lifted Spider from the ground and placed him in the box beside the tomato patch. When the cover was back on the box and the hole covered lightly with straw, they stood in a circle around the hole in the garden. They sang, and they prayed, and they beat on their drums. Everyone said how much he would miss Spider. Everyone was sad.

Spider did not mind spending the day in his box underground. He liked sleeping, and he enjoyed thinking of the trick he was playing on everyone.

Night came. Spider's friends had gone home to the village. His wife and sons were asleep in the banana-leaf house. The full moon was high in the sky. Everything in the garden was quiet.

Can you guess what Spider did then?

Very quietly he lifted the cover of the box. Very quietly he pushed aside the straw which covered the hole and peeped out. He looked round to see that all was safe. When he saw that everyone was in bed, he crawled out very slowly.

The moon was so bright that Spider could see everything in the garden. First he helped himself to the best tomatoes. He helped himself to all the best vegetables growing in the garden.

Even then Spider did not stop. He helped himself to the ripest oranges and bananas. He ended up by going to the hen yard at the back of the garden and helping himself to a fine fat cock.

When he had everything he needed, Spider crawled back into his box and cooked himself a fine dinner. He went on eating for the rest of the night.

The moon disappeared, and the sun came up. Spider did not see what was happening. His full stomach had made him very sleepy. He went on sleeping all through the next day.

The next night, and the next, and the next Spider carried out his plan. How he was enjoying himself! What good things he had to eat in those dinners at night! How he was enjoying his sleeps in the day! What fun it was to fool everyone!

Someone Else Has a Plan

All this time something else was going on which Spider did not know.

Each morning Spider's wife walked out to look at her garden. Each morning she saw that something was very wrong. A thief was stealing her best vegetables. The best oranges and bananas were missing from the trees. Her best cock had disappeared from the hen yard. She must think of a way to catch that thief.

She sat down on a low stool by the door of the banana-leaf house to think. She, too, had a grand idea.

First she gathered a great pile of straw. Out of the straw, she and her two sons made a man that looked just like a real man. Then they got a pail of soft sticky beeswax and covered the straw man from head to foot. They put him in the middle of the tomato patch.

That night, as soon as everyone was asleep, Spider crawled out of his hiding place. He was just about to help himself to a ripe tomato when he saw a man standing in the middle of his garden. He forgot all about being quiet.

"Who are you?" he shouted. "What are you doing in my garden?"

The man did not try to explain. He just stood.

"So you won't answer!" cried Spider. "I'll see about that. I'll change your mind for you."

Still the straw man said nothing.

"Do you think I am joking?" yelled Spider, and with that he hit the straw man with one hand. His hand stuck fast in the beeswax. No matter how hard he pulled, he could not pull his hand away.

"You think you are clever! I'll show you!" shouted Spider. With that, he hit the straw man with his left hand, and that stuck fast too.

"Do you think you can get the better of me?" yelled Spider. He gave a mighty kick with his right foot, and his foot stuck to the straw man too.

"Let me go!" he shouted. "Haven't you learned anything yet? Well then, I'll have to give you another kick."

Spider kicked the straw man again, and that foot stuck too. He kicked and hit until all his hands and feet were stuck fast.

"I'll show you yet!" shouted Spider, and he butted the straw man with his head. There he was, stuck in the beeswax from head to foot.

The next morning his wife and his two sons came out to the garden, hoping to catch the thief. Imagine their surprise when they saw Spider stuck to the straw man. At once they understood everything.

"Thief! Thief!" cried his wife and sons, as they pulled Spider away from the straw man. "Thief! Thief!" they yelled, as they dragged him along with them down to the village.

Soon everyone knew who the thief was. The people laughed at Spider and made up songs about him.

Just as they were about to drag him before the headman of the village to see what should be done with him, Spider broke away from the crowd.

He crawled into a nearby house. He crawled up into the darkest corner under the roof to hide. And he has lived there ever since. And that is why, even today, spiders like to hide in dark corners.

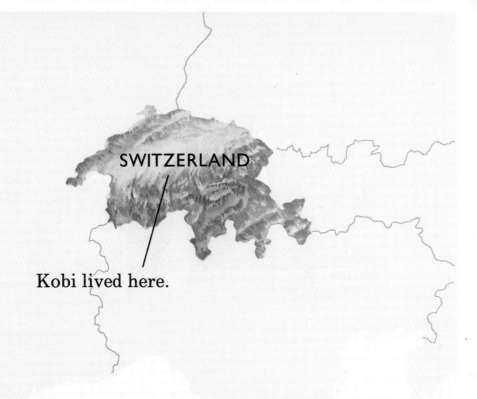

SWITZERLAND

Kobi lived here.

Kobi the Herdboy

A Good Milker

"Kobi, Kobi, if you don't get dressed straight away there won't be any breakfast left for you!"

Mutti's voice rang through the old house. In his room up under the roof Kobi was already sitting on the edge of his bed looking out of the window. Now he pulled on his warm trousers and slipped an old jersey over his head as fast as he could.

Kobi's house was very old. For more than two hundred winters the snow had fallen on it. For more than two hundred summers the sun and rain had beaten against it. They had turned its wooden walls dark brown.

Up the slope behind the house stretched the dark woods. Above the tops of the pine trees Kobi could see the mountain peaks. They were always white with snow, even in the hottest summers.

Kobi hurried down the stairs. He picked up a pail on his way through the kitchen and opened the door that led into the barn.

A sweet smell of hay filled the air. Kobi's grandfather was already at work milking.

"You're late, Kobi," he called. "Gurt thought you weren't coming at all."

Gurt, Kobi's cow, turned her head to look at Kobi. Kobi grabbed his stool and started to milk her. He was slow, but a good milker.

Kobi had been milking cows and goats every day since he was eight years old. Now his thumb and fingers were strong and tough.

When Kobi and Grandfather had finished milking the cows they let them out of the second door to eat the short grass outside. As they carried the milk pails into the kitchen somebody knocked at the door. Kobi ran to open it. There stood his Uncle Jacob.

"Just in time for breakfast, Jacob,"
called Mutti. "Come in and sit down."

"Thank you," said Uncle Jacob. "But
first I have business with Kobi."

He pulled Kobi into a corner and
whispered, "I need a boy to come up
into the Alps this summer to herd and
milk for me. Can you milk?"

Kobi was so excited that he could
hardly speak. He held out his hand.
Uncle Jacob looked at it carefully, and
saw how hard it was.

"That looks good enough," he said.
"Now you will need this." He handed
Kobi a large parcel. Kobi untied the
string, pulled the wrapping off and
looked inside.

"A red jacket! Yellow trousers! This
is a herder's suit! Is it for me, Uncle
Jacob?" yelled Kobi.

"Your little sister can't use it. Your
mother would look funny in it. It is too
small for me now. So it must be for
you," said Uncle Jacob with a laugh.

"One thing I could not find," he went on. "There are no braces there. You must get those for yourself."

Kobi nodded eagerly. He could soon think of a way to get the money for the braces, and perhaps a hat too.

Could he sell his knife? No, that was worth only five francs, and the braces would cost at least twenty. His goat? She was getting too old to climb the mountains, but she was still a good milker. Last year Papa had said she was worth fifty francs. He would sell her at the market, and get his braces.

The Cattle Fair

The sun was just coming up over the mountains as Kobi started down the steep path which joined the road leading to the village. Kobi's lunch was in the rucksack on his back. His goat Blanka trotted along behind him with a rope round her neck.

When he reached the road he found that it was crowded with farmers driving their cattle to market. The bells round the necks of the cows sounded like music.

Boys on bicycles passed by. In their baskets were piglets and hens. Everyone was going to the village to sell something at the fair.

When Kobi reached the market place he could hardly make his way through the noisy crowd of people and animals. At last he found the goat market and tied Blanka safely to a wooden post. There were many other goats there, waiting for a buyer.

Some of the people in the goat market were wearing brightly coloured clothes. Kobi knew that they came from villages far up in the mountains. They were enjoying their day at the market, walking round and making jokes about every animal they saw. Before long they came to Blanka.

One old man stopped in front of her and began to look her over. He opened her mouth to look at her teeth and tell how old she was. He shook his head, and laughed so loudly that his friends came to see what he had found.

"I'll give you twenty francs for her," he said to Kobi. "What do you say to that, boy?"

"Not enough!" cried Kobi. "Papa said that she was worth fifty francs."

"If you ever get fifty francs for that old goat, we will get pink snow," laughed the old man.

"Pink snow," thought Kobi. He had heard Grandfather say that many times. "He means that I will never get fifty francs for Blanka, for snow is never pink."

Nobody else stopped to look at Blanka. Kobi stood first on one foot and then on the other. He was getting bored. He was just beginning to think about taking Blanka home again when he heard a shout.

Kobi looked up in surprise. There in front of him stood his best friend, Sepp. Sepp lived in the same valley as Kobi, and they went to school together.

"What are you doing here?" asked Kobi.

"I came to sell two pigs for my father," said Sepp. "I sold them straight away, and Father said I could have two francs for myself. Are you selling Blanka?"

"I'm trying" said Kobi, "but no one seems to want her." He explained about the herdboy suit, and the money he needed for the braces.

"I thought I could get fifty francs for Blanka, but she must be too old," Kobi finished. "One man said that if I get fifty francs for her there will be pink snow."

"She isn't young," said Sepp, "but she gives a lot of milk."

Blanka was getting restless. She needed to be milked. She kept tugging at the rope that tethered her.

Just then an old man came into the goat market. His hair needed cutting and his hands were dirty. His trousers were so patched that it was hard to tell what colour they were meant to be.

When he saw the two boys standing by their goat he walked up to them. He looked Blanka over. Then he began shouting so loudly that people came to see what was happening.

"This must be the goat Noah took with him on the ark," he shouted.

Quick as a flash Sepp answered,
"Well, those must be Noah's trousers
you have on. You should buy his goat
to go with them."

Everyone laughed. The old man said
no more, but slipped away into the
crowd. Kobi was very glad that Sepp
had been there to answer him.

"What can we do about Blanka?"
he asked Sepp.

"We can milk her now," said Sepp.
"Perhaps somebody will buy her when
they see how much milk she gives."

"That's a good idea!" exclaimed Kobi. "Where can we get a pail?"

"We can borrow one from one of the farmers in the market," said Sepp.

The boys walked back to the cattle market, leaving Blanka tied to the post. In the market they found a farmer who was milking his cows. When he had finished they asked if they might borrow his pail.

On their way back to the goat market the boys forgot about Blanka. They stopped at every stall along the way to see what the people were selling. There were stalls of butter and cheese, flowers and wood carvings.

The boys talked about the coming summer too. Sepp was going up into the mountains with his father's cows. His alp was not far from Uncle Jacob's alp, and the boys could see each other every day.

At last the boys got back to the goat market with the pail. At the very same moment, both of them realized that Blanka had disappeared. She had eaten through the rope that tethered her to the post. Only a small piece of rope was left.

"Blanka has gone!" exclaimed Kobi. "She must have run home to be milked. She's probably there by now. What can we do?"

119

A Greedy Goat

"She won't have gone far," said Sepp. "People always tie up an animal that gets loose. She will be somewhere in the market."

The two boys looked round. Before long they saw a crowd gathered in front of one of the flower stalls. They could hear a woman shouting, and they saw an umbrella going up and down over the heads of the people.

"She must be in there!" cried Kobi.

As quickly as possible the boys pushed their way through the crowd.

Kobi was right. Blanka was there in among the flowers. A woman was holding the end of the rope round Blanka's neck and hitting her with an umbrella as she cried, "You wicked goat! Where is your owner?"

Blanka did not seem to mind the beating. She was still nibbling a flower. People were laughing and encouraging the woman.

As Kobi snatched Blanka's rope from her, the woman shouted, "Why don't you tie your goat up properly? Just look what she has done!"

The woman looked as if she wanted to beat Kobi too, and Sepp quickly stepped between them.

"Why are you beating the goat so hard?" he shouted. "What has she done, anyway?"

"What has she done?" cried the woman, waving her umbrella in the air. "She has eaten all my beautiful flowers. Just look at them! At least six francs' worth have gone. Look for yourself." She pointed to a bucket of flowers at her feet.

Kobi and Sepp looked at the bucket. Blanka had not eaten many flowers, only ten or eleven. She had not had time for more than that.

"Six francs for those few flowers!" shouted Sepp. "You must think your flowers are made of gold!"

The people standing round laughed at that. They thought Sepp was right.

"You tell her, boy!" called one man. "Tell her what her flowers are worth!"

The woman saw that no one was on her side. She turned away crossly.

"Look, we will be fair to you," said Sepp. "We will milk the goat and give you all her milk. That will pay you for the flowers she has eaten."

"Yes, that's fair enough," said the people in the crowd. Even the cross woman agreed. While the crowd began to break up, Kobi gave the rope to Sepp and started to milk Blanka.

An old man who had been in the crowd came over to the boys and watched as the milk started to hit the side of the pail.

After a while he said, "Is your goat a good milker?"

"Yes," answered Kobi. "There is nothing wrong with her except that she is five years old."

"How much do you want for her?" asked the old farmer.

"I have been asking fifty francs," said Kobi.

"That is a great deal of money for a goat who is five years old," said the farmer with a smile.

"Perhaps you think she is worth more because she is your pet? I will give you thirty francs for her. Will you take that?"

Kobi looked up into the kind eyes of the old farmer. Then all at once he found himself telling the farmer all about Uncle Jacob and the herder's suit, and about the leather braces which he must get for himself.

"That is why I have to sell Blanka," Kobi finished.

The farmer smiled and said, "I was once a herdboy on the Alps myself. I still remember how wonderful it was to own my first suit. You will need a hat too, and a gold spoon for your ear. I'll tell you what I'll do. I'll pay you forty francs for your goat. Then you can buy everything you need."

He put forty francs into Kobi's hand and took the rope to lead Blanka off.

As he walked off he turned and said with a smile "Next time you bring a goat to market, use a stronger rope."

"I will," called Kobi, waving to him, as he and Sepp hurried to give the milk to the flower woman. As soon as they had returned the borrowed pail they rushed off down the street to the cobbler's shop.

Kobi put his money down and explained what he wanted. The cobbler pointed to some braces hanging on the wall. Kobi took them down and looked at them. They were beautiful. The brass cows shone like gold on the leather.

A week later a long line of cows, goats and men started up the slopes to the summer pastures.

Far ahead of the others, trying to keep up with a herd of lively goats, was Kobi. He was wearing his herder's suit and his black leather braces, and he was the happiest boy in Switzerland.

ACKNOWLEDGMENTS

Grateful acknowledgment for permission to use or adapt material is made to:

Little, Brown and Company, for an approved adaptation of *The Adventures of Spider* by Joyce Cooper Arkhurst

Parnassus Press, for an adaptation of *Ramon Makes a Trade* by Barbara Ritchie

The Viking Press, Inc., for an adaptation from *Kobi* by Mary and Conrad Buff

Published by James Nisbet & Co. Ltd
Digswell Place, Welwyn, Herts.
Made and printed by William Clowes & Sons, Ltd
London, Beccles and Colchester
First Edition 1974